# Dinosaur on Hanukkah

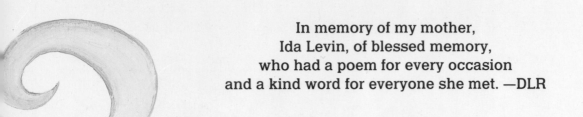

In memory of my mother,
Ida Levin, of blessed memory,
who had a poem for every occasion
and a kind word for everyone she met. —DLR

# Dinosaur on Hanukkah

Diane Levin Rauchwerger

pictures by Jason Wolff

KAR-BEN
PUBLISHING

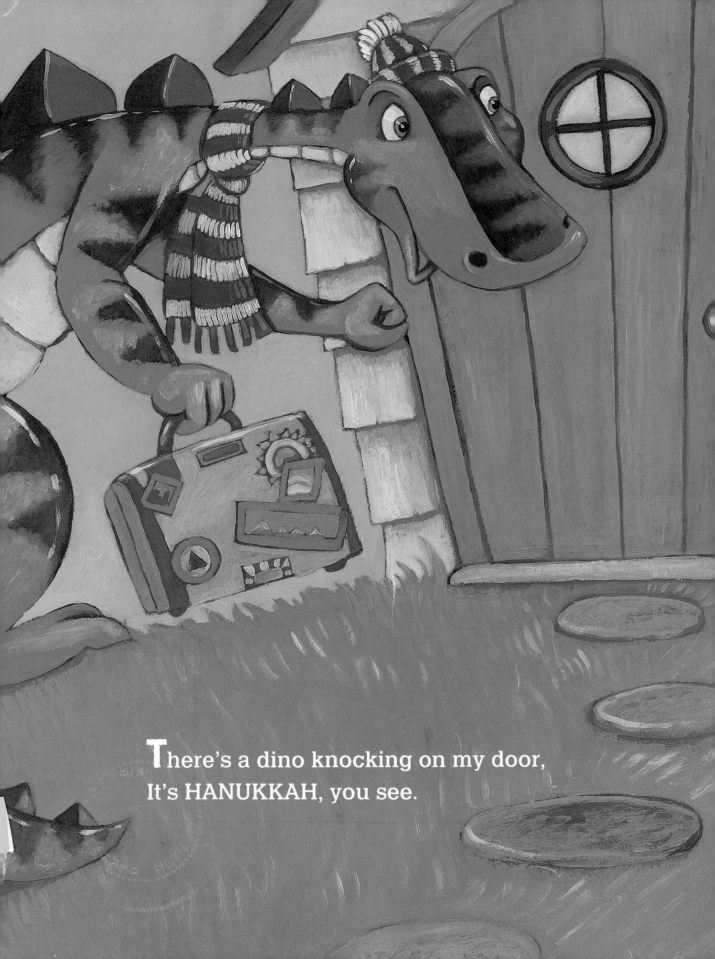

There's a dino knocking on my door,
It's HANUKKAH, you see.

He's come to decorate our house
And celebrate with me.

He marches all around the room
As brave as brave can be,
Acting out the ancient tale
Of Judah Maccabee.

He helps me wrap some presents
With ribbons and with bows.

I have a special gift for him—
I'm pretty sure he knows.

I've hidden it behind the door,
My closet's much too full.
I've bought him a new sweater
Of fluffy, purple wool.

He has a yummy gift for me,
Chocolate gelt so sweet.
But didn't know that
it could melt . . .

. . . It's oozing down his feet!

He gobbles up the latkes,
And juggles them for fun.
There's batter on the walls and floor
Before I say, "We're done."

He needs help
lighting candles,
He knows each night
there's more.

But once he's lit
the shamash,
He can only count
to four.

He drips wax on the counter,
Knocks matches on the floor,

He's making such an awful mess
I show him to the door.

He's back to play the dreidel game—
Nun, gimmel, hey, and shin—
But he pouts so when he loses
I just have to let him win.

When Hanukkah is over,
I give his tail a tweak.
"Don't wait a year to celebrate—
Shabbat comes every week!"

**On Hanukkah,** an eight-day Festival of Lights, Jews celebrate the victory of the Maccabees over the mighty armies of the Syrian king Antiochus. When they restored the Holy Temple in Jerusalem, the Maccabees found one jug of pure oil, enough to keep the menorah burning for just one day. But, according to the story, a miracle happened and the oil burned for eight days. On each night of the holiday an additional candle is added to the menorah, which is lit with the *shamash*, the helper candle. It is traditional to exchange gifts, eat foods fried in oil—*latkes* (potato pancakes) and *sufganiyot* (donuts)—and play the dreidel game. A dreidel is a spinning top. The letters on its four sides are nun, gimmel, hey, and shin, which stand for "A Great Miracle Happened There."

Text copyright © 2005 by Diane Levin Rauchwerger
Illustrations copyright © 2005 by Jason Wolff

KAR-BEN PUBLISHING, INC.
A division of Lerner Publishing Group
241 First Avenue North
Minneapolis, MN 55401 U.S.A.
800-4KARBEN

Website address: www.karben.com

Library of Congress Cataloging-in-Publication Data

Rauchwerger, Diane Levin.
    Dinosaur on Hanukkah / by Diane Levin
Rauchwerger ; illustrations by Jason Wolff.
        p.   cm.
    Summary: A dinosaur comes to a young boy's
house to join him in celebrating Hanukkah.
    ISBN: 1—58013—145—X (lib. bdg. : alk. paper)
    [1. Hanukkah—Fiction.  2. Dinosaurs—Fiction.
3. Stories in rhyme.]  I. Wolff, Jason, ill.  II. Title.
PZ8.3.R2323Di 2005
[E]—dc22                              2004014266

Manufactured in the United States of America
1 2 3 4 5 6 − DP − 10 09 08 07 06 05